This **Frog** book belongs **to:**

....

For Viktor

This paperback edition first published in 2014 by Andersen Press Ltd.
20 Vauxhall Bridge Road, London SW1V 2SA.
First published in Great Britain in 2001 by Andersen Press Ltd.
Published in Australia by Random House Australia Pty.,
20 Alfred Street, Milsons Point, Sydney, NSW 2061.
Copyright © Foundation Max Velthuijs, 2001.
The rights of Max Velthuijs to be identified as the author and illustrator
of this work have been asserted by him in accordance with the
Copyright, Designs and Patents Act, 1988.
All rights reserved.
Colour separated in Switzerland by Photolitho AG, Zürich.
Printed and bound in China.

10   9   8   7   6   5   4   3

British Library Cataloguing in Publication Data available.
ISBN 978 1 78344 150 1

Frog
Finds
a Friend

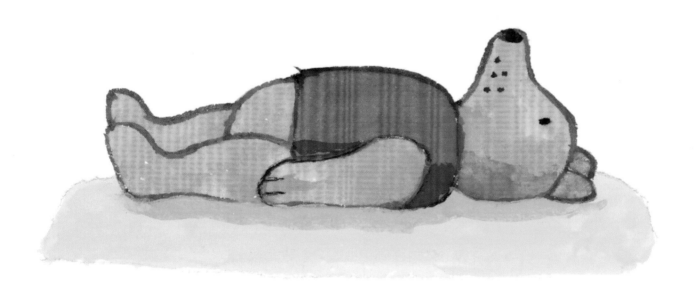

Max Velthuijs

Andersen Press

It was a fine autumn day. Frog was wandering through the woods, looking at the colours of the leaves on the trees – golden-yellow, orange and brown.

"The world is truly beautiful," he thought.

All at once, amidst the wonderful colours, he caught sight of something else wonderful lying in the grass . . .

He went up closer, and saw that it was a little brown bear wearing a red sweater. It had beady black eyes and there was a teardrop on its cheek.

Tenderly, Frog picked it up. "Oh, how lovely he is,"
he thought. "I shall take him back to my house and
he can live with me."
Hugging him close to his chest, Frog carried his
new little friend homewards . . .

They met Pig on the way.

"What have you got there?" asked Pig.
"My new friend," said Frog. "I found him in the woods.
"But what will you do with him?" said Pig.
"He's going to live with me. Because he is all alone,"
said Frog.

"Let me see him," said Hare, who had overheard.
"Why, it's just a teddybear," he exclaimed. "A *toy*.
It can't even talk!"
"I'm going to teach him," said Frog.

And hand in hand, Frog and the little bear walked to Frog's house. The little bear could walk very well.

For the first few days, the little bear said nothing.
But he ate a lot. He had a very good appetite!

Before going to sleep, Frog told the little bear
fairytales and taught him words such as apple,
rose, moon . . .

During the day, they played lots of football and many other interesting games.

And in the evenings, they painted beautiful pictures. They had a lovely time together and so, little by little, Bear began to talk.

One day, Frog asked him, "Where exactly do you come from, Little Bear?"
"Over there," said Bear. And he pointed with his paw.

Hare overheard them talking. He was amazed.
"Can he really talk?" he asked.
"Of course," said Frog proudly. "I taught him."

Everyone came running to hear this incredible thing.
"Can you really talk, Little Bear?" they all asked together
"Say something!"
For a moment all was quiet, and then: "Good morning.
What lovely weather we're having," said Bear.
At that they all burst out laughing.

From that day on, all the animals spoiled the little bear.
Duck let him ride around on her back . . .

Pig baked him special Bear Cookies from her very own *Bear Cookie* recipe . . .

and even Rat was happy to take him fishing
with him.
They all adored Bear and Bear loved every minute.

But the day came, quite unexpectedly, when Bear just sat on a rock staring into the distance.

He didn't want to play anymore and he wouldn't
speak to anyone . . .

and at dinner time he didn't want to eat anything.
"Little Bear," asked Frog, "what's wrong? Don't you feel
well? Are you sick?"
"No," replied Bear, quietly. "I don't know what it is."

But the next morning, he was up very early.
"Where are you going?" asked Frog anxiously.
"I'm going back," said Bear. "Back to where I came
from, where I belong."

The other animals ran up to see what was happening.

"Are you going away?" they asked, shocked.
"Where to?"
"Do you know the way?"
"I'll find it," said Bear.
There was no doubt about it. He really was leaving.

Sadly they filled a little rucksack with food and drink to last him the journey. Then Bear started out, back to where he had come from.

Frog was heartbroken. That night, and the nights
that followed, he lay in bed, tossing and turning
with grief. "Oh, Little Bear, I *miss* you so!" he wept,
and he cried himself to sleep.
Then one morning, very early, something warm
and soft climbed into bed next to him . . .

Frog opened his eyes. "Little Bear," he whispered, "have you come back? Can it really be you?"

"Yes," said Bear. "You are my dearest friend and I belong *here*, with you. I know that now and I never want to go away again."

And with that, Frog and Bear went happily to sleep.

Max Velthuijs's twelve beautiful stories about **Frog** and his friends first started to appear twenty five years ago and are now available as paperbacks, e-books and apps.

9781783441440

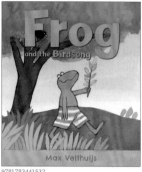
9781783441532

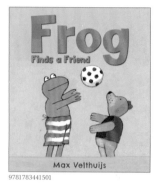
9781783441501

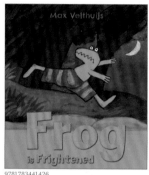
9781783441426

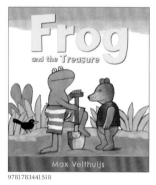
9781783441471

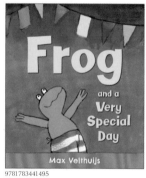
9781783441457

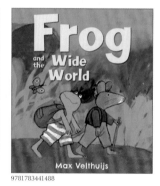
9781783441525

97811783441433

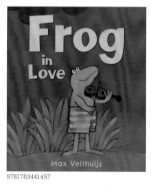
9781783441518

9781783441495

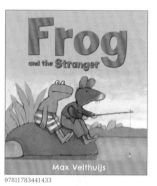
9781783441488

9781783441419

Max Velthuijs (Dutch for Field House) lived in the Netherlands, and received the prestigious Hans Christian Andersen Medal for Illustration. His charming stories capture childhood experiences while offering life lessons to children as young as three, and have been translated into more than forty languages.

'Frog is an inspired creation – a masterpiece of graphic simplicity.' GUARDIAN

'Miniature morality plays for our age.' IBBY